Storybook ABCs

By Meg McLaughlin   Illustrated by

D1379095

Dalmatian Press, LLC, 2008. All rights reserved.
Published by Dalmatian Press, LLC, 2008. The DALMATIAN PRESS name and logo are trademarks of Dalmatian Press, LLC, Franklin, Tennessee 37067. No part of this book may be reproduced or copied in any form without written permission from the copyright owner.
Printed in the U.S.A.
ISBN: 1-40375-018-1 (X)

08 09 10 B&M 10 9 8 7 6 5 4 3 2 1
17376 Sesame Street 8x8 Storybook: Storybook ABCs

D
Dog

Cowabunga!

Hey, diddle-diddle,
The cat and the fiddle,
The cow jumped over the *mooooooon*.
The little dog laughed to see such sport,
And the dish ran away with the spoon.

That was a doozie
of a candy!

G
Goose

Old Mother Goose,
When she wanted to wander,
Would glide o'er the garden
Upon a grand gander.

Goodness gwacious!
Take a gander at that!

J
Jack

Jog and juggle! Jack, be quick!
Jack, jump over the candlestick!

Enough jogging, juggling,
and jumping. I, Jack, am
going back to beanstalks.

L

Lamb

Prairie had a little lamb,
Little lamb, little lamb.
Prairie had a little lamb.
Its fleece was light as snow.

Messy Miss Muffet
Sat on a tuffet,
Eating some mud soufflé.
In marched a spider
To sit down beside her—
But she frightened that spider away!

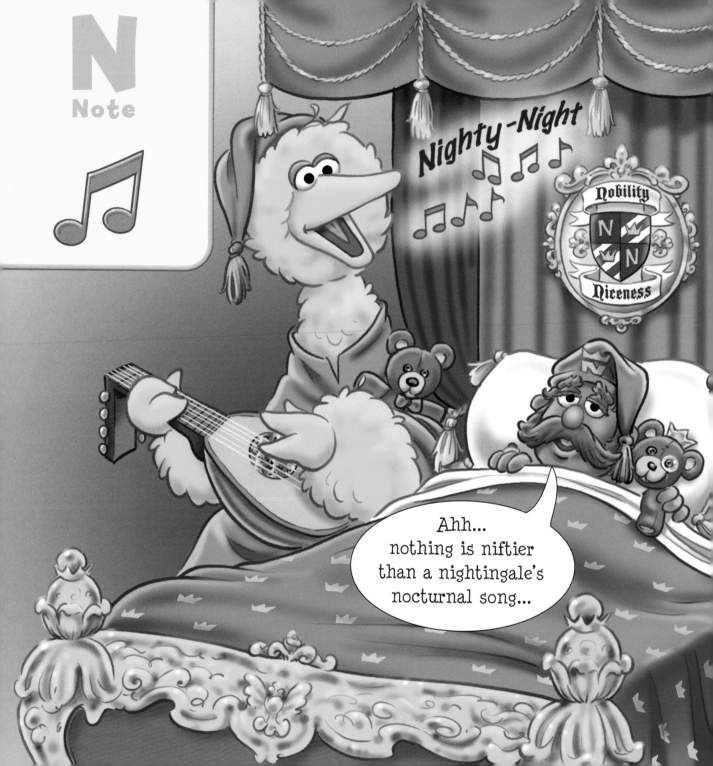

Q
Queen

Oh, I quit.

The Queen of Hearts
Made quiche and tarts,
All on a quiet day.
The Knave of Hearts,
He stole those tarts
And quickly ran away!